And God Created Squash

HOW THE WORLD BEGAN

Martha Whitmore Hickman

Illustrated by Giuliano Ferri

ALBERT WHITMAN & COMPANY • MORTON GROVE, ILLINOIS

The text typeface is Caxton Book.
The illustration media are
watercolor and colored pencil.
Design by Karen Johnson Campbell.

Text © 1993 by Martha Whitmore Hickman.
Illustrations © 1993 by Giuliano Ferri.
Published in 1993 by Albert Whitman & Company,
6340 Oakton Street, Morton Grove, Illinois 60053.
Printed in U.S.A. All rights reserved.
10 9 8 7 6 5 4 3 2 1

Library of Congress Cataloging-in-Publication Data
Hickman, Martha Whitmore.
And God created squash : how the world began /
Martha Whitmore Hickman ; illustrated by
Giuliano Ferri.
p.   cm.
Summary: As God thinks about light and darkness,
water and land, plants and animals—and people—
the world is created.
ISBN 0-8075-0340-1
[1. Creation—Fiction.] I. Ferri, Giuliano, ill.
II. Title.
PZ7.H53143An   1993   92-22654
[E]—dc20   CIP
                                             AC

In the beginning was God.

Nothing but God.

Then it was as though God took a deep breath . . .

and held it . . .

and let it go.

And there was the universe!

"So far, so good!" God said.

At first, the universe was all darkness and swirling water. No shape to anything. Nothing belonging anywhere.

God looked out over all the darkness and water. "I'd like something to go with the darkness," God said. "How about . . . light?

"Good idea," God thought. And God made light.

So now there was light as well as darkness. "I'll call the light 'day,' " God said. "And I'll call the darkness 'night.' That's good," God said.

Then God said, "I'll divide the water and put some up above, for rain and snow and hail, and some down below, for oceans and lakes and rivers and ponds and puddles at the edges of sidewalks—if I decide to have sidewalks."

So there was water up above and water down below. "And in between the water above and the water below, I'll put the sky," God said.

Then God collected the water under the sky in great, deep oceans—except for a little God saved for lakes and rivers and ponds. And where the water had been was now . . . land. "I'll call the land 'Earth,'" God said.

"Earth," God said again, and liked the sound of it.
God put an ear down to the earth, but there wasn't
much happening. "I'd like to hear something growing,"
God said.

So God drew a deep breath and held it. "How about plants?" God thought. And there appeared on the earth plants.

"What shall I call them?" God wondered. "Maybe . . . wheat and barley and rice and corn."

God took another breath. "How about . . . yellow apples and plums with purple skins and small grapes to turn into raisins. . . . But I'm getting ahead of myself," thought God.

"And how about something long and green, with little strings along the side? . . . Beans!" God said. "And how about . . . squash?

"I like that name," God said. "I think I'll use it again. Acorn squash. Butternut squash. Even zucchini squash. I might have a game and call it squash. Or put my hand on something and press down hard and call that squash," God said. "And I'll have flowers—daisies and poppies and perfumed lilies—to make the world smell sweet.

"That's very good," God said. "I like what I have made so far."

And then God wondered, "How will I show when it's daytime or nighttime—time to walk in the dewy grass or time to catch fireflies?"

So God made the sun, very bright, for daytime, and the moon, much dimmer, for night. And whirling planets. And then some stars to scatter over the sky. "For a little extra light," God said. "And just to make it pretty."

"I wonder what to make next,"
God thought. "I don't have
anything swimming or jumping or
flashing through the water. . . . How
about sting rays and whales and
clams, trout and salmon and bass?
And polliwogs," God said. "How
about polliwogs? And jellyfish—not
to be confused with another kind
of jelly I might make later."

And so fish and other sea
creatures began to glisten and glide.
God said, "You are to mate and
produce offspring to fill the lakes
and rivers and oceans and dart
in and out of deep caves at the
bottom of the sea."

Then God said, "How about something that will fly around . . . with maybe little flapping side pieces, and beaks to hold food and gather string and pluck twigs from my plants? How about . . . birds?" God said, and lo and behold, birds flew in the sky.

God smiled. "I like that! If I weren't God, I might choose to be a bird."

Then God said to the birds, "Birds, I want you to mate and lay eggs—blue and brown and yellow eggs—so there will be lots of birds. Please?"

And the birds went flying off into the sky, singing their songs. "Good idea—birds," said God.

"Now," God said, "I'd like some creatures to walk and run and leap on this beautiful earth that I have made. How about a creature with a slender body and a big, curly mane? I'm thinking . . . lion," God said.

"And then I'm thinking buffalo and tiger and sheep. And something huge and gray with a long, swinging trunk for carrying food and for spraying water.

"I'm thinking elephant!" said God.

"And then I'm thinking turtle
and lizard and mouse and tree toad
and snake and porcupine . . . and
sloth, for resting. And I'm thinking
ants and spiders and caterpillars,
and who knows what else I might
think of when I get around to it,"
God said. "But now . . ."

And then God drew an enormous
breath and held it for a long time,
thinking and thinking.

"All that I have made is splendid,"
God said. "But something's missing.
I'm lonesome. I'd like some company.
How about something . . . well,
more like me?

"I've got it!" God said. "People!
Men and women and boys and girls
and small babies for the boys and
girls to hold and sing to and help
take care of . . ."

And slowly God let out a long
breath, and there appeared a man
and a woman.

"Well!" God said. "Bless you!
I have big plans for you."

Then God said, "I'd like you to
have children. You and your
children shall care for the earth —
for the plants and the fish, the birds
and the animals. There is food
enough for all of you if you use
my creation wisely."

And in what seemed no time at all, there were upon the earth men and women and boys and girls, babies and aunts and uncles and cousins, grandmothers and grandfathers and farmers and teachers, beekeepers and doctors and lifeguards and sculptors, bus drivers and flute players and jugglers

and cooks, carpenters and firefighters and mayors of cities.

And God said, "Attention, please! May I have your attention?"

Some people were quiet right away, and some were so excited that they took awhile to be still.

"Welcome," God said. "You are my most ambitious creation. You are a lot like me. I have given you power. Not to mention a brain. I hope you are happy, and that you love the world I have made. *I* do—it is quite wonderful."

God waited. "Are there any questions?"

Everyone was so pleased and surprised to be alive that there weren't any questions.

"Well, you may have questions later," God said. "If you do, ask me. We can at least think about them together."

God looked around. "Now it's time for a day of rest," God said. "For me, too.

"But if you want me, speak my name. Remember, I made you for company, for me and for each other. So we could love each other. And I will never forget you.

"I'll be around. You may not see
me. But I'll be here—and there—
wherever you are, whenever you need
me. Even in the middle of the night.
"Think of me. I'll be thinking
of you."